Red Stocking Rescue

Kate Saunders worked as an actress until she was twenty-five and then became a writer. She has written five novels and edited a collection of short stories. As a journalist she has worked for the *Sunday Times*, the *Daily Telegraph*, the *Independent* and the *Sunday Express*, and is currently writing a weekly column in the *Express*. She can be heard regularly on BBC Radio 4, presenting *Woman's Hour* and appearing on *Start the Week* and *Front Row*. She lives in London and has a six-year-old son.

The *Belfry Witches* titles are Kate's first books for children. A major BBC TV series is based on them.

All Belfry Witches titles can be ordered at
your local bookshop or are available by post
from Book Service by Post (tel: 01624 675137).

The Belfry Witches

Red Stocking Rescue

Kate Saunders
Illustrated by Tony Ross

MACMILLAN
CHILDREN'S BOOKS

For Dylan and Rowan

First published 1999 by Macmillan Children's Books
a division of Macmillan Publishers Limited
25 Eccleston Place, London SW1W 9NF
Basingstoke and Oxford
www.macmillan.co.uk

Associated companies throughout the world

ISBN 0 330 37284 X

1 3 5 7 9 8 6 4 2

A CIP catalogue record for this book is available from
the British Library.

Typeset by SX Composing DTP, Rayleigh, Essex
Printed and bound in Great Britain by Mackays of Chatham plc, Kent

Contents

1

An Announcement

"You may now open the oven," Mendax said, "very gently so your cake doesn't sink. It's supposed to be a Victoria sponge – not a Victoria pancake!"

"Stop fussing!" growled Skirty Marm.

"Do as he says," urged Old Noshie. "You know we're rubbish at making cakes by ourselves!"

The vicarage kitchen at Tranters End was filled with a delicious smell of baking. It was also filled with a collection of characters you wouldn't normally expect to find in a vicarage.

Mendax was a small black cat. He was standing on his hind legs on the kitchen table. A flowered apron was tied round his waist, and his tail was tucked into the pocket to keep it out of the way. Old Noshie and Skirty Marm were two genuine witches, in black pointed hats and musty rags.

The witches had been pressing their noses against the oven door for the past half hour – and Mendax had been nagging them not to peep. The moment he gave his permission, the impatient pair opened the oven and carefully took out a round cake tin (they didn't need oven gloves, and they didn't burn their noses, because leathery witch-skin is not as delicate as the human sort).

"*Perfect!*" purred Mendax as the witches put the cake tin down on the cooling rack beside him. He tested the surface of the cake with his paw. "Nice golden colour, beautifully light, lovely smell – now, aren't you glad you followed my instructions?"

"Our first Victoria sponge," Skirty Marm said solemnly. It was such a great moment that she'd decided not to mind taking orders from a cat.

"Cor," murmured Old Noshie, "isn't it beautiful?"

The cake was for their best friend, Mr Babbercorn, who was coming home from his holiday that afternoon. He'd been away for two whole weeks.

Mendax sighed. "Poor Mr B., he works so hard. I do hope he's had a nice restful time."

"*We* certainly haven't," Skirty Marm said crossly. "And neither has the vicar. You've done nothing but boss, boss, boss, Mendax. I can't wait for Mr B. to come back and shut you up."

"Nonsense," said Mendax smugly. "He'll thank me for my splendid management."

Cuthbert Babbercorn was the curate at St Tranter's Church. A series of amazing adventures had brought the witches and Mendax to the sleepy English village of Tranters End. There had been some troublesome incidents at first, but the local people were now quite used to having witches in the church belfry and a rather bossy, talking cat at the vicarage.

These days, everyone in the village understood that although Old Noshie and Skirty Marm were ancient by human standards – over a hundred and fifty years old – they were very young for witches. The villagers had learned to make allowances for this unusual situation, and the witches had joined both the Brownies and the Old Folks' Drop-In Club. They often argued about which one they liked best. Skirty Marm liked singing with the Old Folks and hearing their interesting stories about human history. Old Noshie, less intellectual than her friend, preferred a brisk game of rounders with the Brownies.

Skirty Marm was tall and skinny, with a ragged mop of purple hair, a wrinkled grey face and gleaming red eyes. At witch school (as she was always reminding Old Noshie) she had been top of the class in everything. She had won the Spellbinder's Medal for thirty-six years in a row, plus two Golden Brooms for stunt flying, and the coveted Spitting Shield, not to mention various other prizes.

Old Noshie had never won anything except a Highly Commended badge for growing mould on a flannel. She was a short round witch, with bright green skin that glowed in the dark. Her wrinkled old head was as bald as an egg, and she usually wore a blue wig to keep it warm. She had great respect for Skirty Marm's wisdom and followed her in everything – which was not always a very good idea.

Both witches had picked up various human customs during their time in Tranters End, but there was one witchy thing they couldn't give up. Under their rags, each of them wore a pair of sagging, holey red stockings. They had been stripped of their official stockings when they left Witch Island, their old home, but their great friend Mrs Tucker, who ran the village post office and was also Brown Owl, had thrilled them by giving them new pairs.

I must explain that on Witch Island, where Skirty Marm and Old Noshie had grown up, you can tell a witch's age and importance by the colour of her stockings.

Yellow-Stockings are baby witches, studying basic magic at school. When they reach the age of one hundred, they become Red-Stockings and receive the Red-Stocking Spellbook. At the age of two hundred, they become Green-Stockings and are entitled to cast far stronger spells. Finally, at the age of three hundred, they become Purple-Stockings, the most powerful witches of all.

During Noshie and Skirty's time on Witch Island, the Purple-Stockings had been allowed to keep cat-slaves and to treat the younger witches like servants. The unfairness of it had driven the young Red-Stockings crazy. They hadn't dared disobey, however, because they lived in terror of the queen, Mrs Abercrombie.

This monstrous witch was nearly a thousand years old, hideously ugly and fiendishly clever.

Old Noshie and Skirty Marm would never have come to Tranters End in the first place if they hadn't sung a very rude song about Mrs Abercrombie at the Hallowe'en Ball. The furious old queen had banished them from the island. She might have forgotten about the song in a hundred years or so, but Old Noshie and Skirty Marm had since committed two far greater crimes. First, they had helped to lead a Red-Stocking revolution on the island, which had freed the cat-slaves and ended Mrs Abercrombie's cruel reign. Second – and far more serious – they had stolen the Power Hat.

The Power Hat was two metres tall, and an everlasting candle burned at its point. It was tremendously magical. No living witch knew how to awaken all its powers, but the witch who owned it became the strongest in the world. Without the Power Hat, Mrs Abercrombie was a fiendishly clever but ordinary Purple-Stocking, and only a few of her friends had voted for her when the first Witch Island elections were held after the Red-Stocking revolution. When last heard of, she was living in a small retirement-cave on the coast, casting spells to find the Power Hat and plotting her revenge.

Old Noshie and Skirty Marm hoped with all their hearts that the wicked ex-queen would never find the Power Hat. Mrs Abercrombie had recently written her memoirs (*My Stormy Passage*, Belch & Squelch, 10 witch shillings) and there was a whole chapter called "What I Will do to Old Noshie and Skirty Marm When I Get My Hat Back".

The two witches and Mr Babbercorn had hidden the Power Hat in the foundations of the new extension to the village hall at Tranters End. It had stayed there, perfectly peacefully, for over a year. Skirty Marm, however, was worried.

"I need to ask Mr B.'s advice about the you-know-what," she told Mendax and Old Noshie now. "I don't like what's happening at the village hall."

"Pish and posh," Old Noshie said gaily. "He'll be pleased with the changes."

While Mr Babbercorn was away on his holiday, there had been some peculiar goings-on. The hollyhocks outside the village hall had grown huge, with flowers the size of tubas. The terrible, tuneless church choir, which practised at the hall, had suddenly begun to sing like angels – only the week before, they had won first prize at a choir festival.

"I don't like it," Skirty Marm repeated, shaking her head. "It means the Hat's getting restless – and if it gives itself away, Mrs Abercrombie will find it."

"Oh, stop fretting," Old Noshie said. "Everything's fine – and we've just made a wonderful cake."

"A jolly good effort!" declared Mendax. His whiskers lifted in a smug smile. "Did I ever tell you about the sponge I baked under cannon fire at the Battle of Fungus Gulch?"

The witches groaned and rudely blew raspberries. In Latin, "Mendax" means *liar*, and the name suited this former cat-slave down to the tip of his glossy tail. He was absolutely addicted to telling tall stories.

Like all great liars, though, Mendax was very offended when people accused him of lying. "Not one of my best sponges, obviously," he said huffily. "I didn't have time to fold in the eggs. Would you like me to ice your cake?"

"Thanks, Mendax," said Old Noshie, "and could you write 'Welcome Home Mr B.' on it?"

"With pleasure. I know your spelling would never stand the strain."

"None of your cheek!" snapped Skirty Marm. Unlike the easy-going Old Noshie, she could never forget that Mendax had once been a spy, sent by Mrs Abercrombie to destroy them.

"Come on, Skirt," Old Noshie said quickly, "let's pick some nice weeds to decorate the tea table."

This had been Mr Babbercorn's first real holiday for years, and Old Noshie didn't want his homecoming to be spoiled by squabbling. Skirty allowed Noshie to drag her into the

garden. They gathered a fine bunch of dandelions, bindweed and thistles.

While the witches were arranging their weeds on the table, the vicar of St Tranter's Church, Mr Snelling, smelt cake and came out of his study. He was a smiling, roly-poly man, who was very fond of food.

"Oh, witches! What a spread!" he cried. "Victoria sponge cake, egg sandwiches *and* fairy cakes – and what's in these rolls?"

"Spiders," said Old Noshie, smacking her lips hungrily. "Fresh this morning. Do try one."

Mr Snelling made a face. "No thanks. I think I'll try a fairy cake."

"Leave those alone!" Mendax mewed sternly. "You don't get a bite to eat until you've finished writing your sermon!"

The vicar sighed. "You've got dreadfully above yourself, Mendax. I can't wait till Babbercorn comes home. He's the only person who can keep you in order!"

Mr Babbercorn had gone away a thin, pale, weedy young man. He returned with a healthy tan and fashionable new glasses.

"Cuthbert, you look simply wonderful," the

vicar said, with his mouth full of fairy cake. "Ah, there's nothing like the seaside. Gusty Bay must be a very refreshing place."

"It's a beautiful spot," said Mr Babbercorn. He heaved a deep sigh and smiled dreamily.

Mr Snelling was too busy eating to notice anything odd about Mr Babbercorn's behaviour, and the witches were too busy admiring the boxes of Gusty Bay fudge their friend had just given them.

"Eat up, Cuthbert!" cried Mr Snelling. "You haven't touched this excellent tea!"

Mr Babbercorn sighed again and helped himself to a spider roll. He would have taken a bite if Mendax hadn't snatched it out of his hand.

For the first time the vicar looked properly at Mr Babbercorn. "Cuthbert, what on earth is the matter with you? Ever since you arrived, we've had nothing from you but sighs and cheesy smiles."

Mr Babbercorn's face slowly blushed the colour of a radish. "I . . . I . . . I . . ." he stammered. "The fact is . . . I have an announcement."

He paused. The witches and Mendax waited

11

open-mouthed. Mr Snelling had frozen with a fairy cake halfway to his lips.

"The fact is," the young curate said in a rush, "I'M GETTING MARRIED."

There was a moment of stunned silence before the vicar threw the fairy cake into the air with a shriek of joy. "My dear Cuthbert, how romantic! Oh, what heavenly news!"

"HURRAH!" yelled Old Noshie and Skirty Marm. They were longing to see a human wedding – there was no such thing on Witch Island.

"Dear me," said Mendax, a faraway look in his bright green eyes. "Did I ever tell you about my little romance? It was spring in Paris, we were young and foolish – poor Fifi!"

The vicar giggled. "Do stop lying, Mendax. I want to hear all about the future Mrs Babbercorn!"

Back came the curate's dreamy smile. "Her name's Alice Wisk. I met her on the beach when she got her leg stuck in a deckchair. She works in a library and she's the prettiest, cleverest, kindest girl in the whole world!"

"Have you got a picture of her?" asked Old Noshie eagerly.

Mr Babbercorn had indeed got a picture of Alice. He took it carefully out of his pocket and showed it to his friends with bashful pride. The snap was of a sweet-faced young woman with curly brown hair and a lovely smile. She was sitting on a giant toadstool in a park, eating a "99" ice cream.

"Charming!" declared the vicar, with a sigh of delight. "Quite charming!"

Skirty Marm peered at the photograph and gasped, "She's as beautiful as a princess – I can't wait to see her in her white dress!"

"It's a shame you can't wear one too," Old Noshie told Mr Babbercorn. "You'd look great."

Mr Babbercorn laughed. "I'm afraid only the bride gets the white dress."

Mr Snelling cut himself a large slice of sponge cake. "Do you know," he said, "I've often wondered why you don't have weddings on Witch Island. I mean – where do little witches come from?"

"We're grown from seed," explained Skirty Marm. "We get our Yellow-Stockings as soon as we're ready to leave the potting sheds. It's not like humans at all."

"Not at all," agreed the vicar and the curate.

Old Noshie was still gazing at the photograph. "When can we meet Alice?"

"Oh," said Mr Babbercorn, "ah."

His face, which had been so red, turned white. "She's coming to Tranters End next week – but there's a slight problem."

"What problem?" asked the vicar.

Mr Babbercorn hung his head. "I haven't exactly told her about the magic."

Mr Snelling groaned. "Oh, Cuthbert!"

"Well, it'll be a nice surprise for her," said Old Noshie happily. "Perhaps we can do a few little spells to make her feel welcome."

"No!" squeaked Mr Babbercorn, horrified.

"You really should have mentioned something before you invited her here," said Mr Snelling.

"I know," sighed Mr Babbercorn, "but there was never a right moment. How on earth do you tell the woman of your dreams that you live with two witches and a talking cat?"

"I can see it might be tricky," Mr Snelling admitted.

"Anyone would think," said Mendax coldly, "that you were *ashamed* of us."

"Oh, please don't think that!" Mr Babbercorn cried. "You're all my dear friends, and I know Alice will love you as much as I do. But, can't you see – I have to warn her about you first!"

Old Noshie was frowning. "I suppose so," she said grudgingly. "She might be scared of witches."

Mr Babbercorn looked pleadingly at his three magical friends. "Just at the beginning," he said, in a hesitant and embarrassed voice, "just to start with, I'd be very grateful if you witches would stay out of sight – and if Mendax could behave like an ordinary cat."

"*Ordinary!*" Mendax shuddered.

"I'll tell her as soon as she's settled in, honestly!"

"All right," Old Noshie said crossly. "We'll stay out of sight – won't we, Skirt? Just at first."

Mr Babbercorn looked hard at Skirty Marm. "Do you promise?"

"Oh, I promise," Skirty Marm said distantly.

Only Old Noshie noticed that Skirty Marm had her fingers crossed.

2

Dear Old Souls

Mr Babbercorn was a popular young curate. The announcement that he was getting married filled the people of Tranters End with delight. Everyone was longing to meet Alice Wisk.

"Her first day here will be quite a social whirl," Mendax told the witches on the morning of Alice's visit. "Lunch with the churchwardens, tea at the Old Folks' Drop-In Club, a visit to the Brownies, and dinner with the bishop." He licked his paw gloomily. "And they won't even let me help with the food! I have to sit in the sun, rub myself against people's legs, play with stupid toys—"

He broke off, shuddering. "I simply *loathe* behaving like an ordinary cat. I'll completely lose the respect of the mice."

"We're Brownies *and* Old Folk!" sniffed Old Noshie. "It's MEAN not to invite us! I would have thought Alice would be pleased to meet two nice witches. She might ask us to be her bridesmaids!" Old Noshie longed to be a bridesmaid.

"And if she was allowed to hear my voice," said Mendax, "I'm sure she'd *beg* me to sing a solo at her wedding."

Skirty Marm was in a rage. She stormed around the church belfry where she and Old Noshie lived, raising a cloud of dust from the splintery wooden floorboards.

"It's just NOT FAIR!" she shouted. "It

would serve that mean, stinky, selfish curate right if we—"

The rest of her speech was drowned out by a tremendous "CLANG!" which made the whole belfry shake. The church clock was striking twelve, and the two enormous bells made a deafening racket. Mendax turned pale under his black fur and streaked away down the one hundred and eighty-six belfry steps. The witches, however, rather liked the noise.

When it was over, Old Noshie said, "Sorry, Skirt – I didn't quite catch that."

Skirty Marm's red eyes were dangerously thoughtful. "I've just had one of my ideas," she said.

"Have you?" Old Noshie tried not to sound dismayed. Skirty Marm's ideas usually led straight to trouble.

"Listen," said Skirty Marm. "Mr B. doesn't want Alice to meet witches. Right?"

"You know it is, Skirt – in case she changes her mind about marrying him."

"Suppose we're *not* witches?" Skirty Marm smiled craftily. "Suppose we're just ordinary members of the Old Folks' Club? We could join them for tea at the vicarage, and Mr B. wouldn't have any excuse to throw us out. Besides, it would make it easier to tell Alice about us when the right time comes!"

Skirty Marm was getting excited as the flame of her genius burned higher. "He'd only have to say something like, 'Alice, remember those two old ladies from the Drop-In Club? Well, they're witches.' *Simple!*"

Old Noshie's green face was doubtful. "It'd never work. Alice would notice our pointed hats straight away."

Skirty Marm gave her friend a quick biff on the head. This sometimes helped Old Noshie to organize her muddled thoughts.

"You silly old bag, that's the whole point! We wouldn't be wearing our hats! We'd be disguised as two REAL OLD LADIES!"

The boldness and brilliance of this plan took Old Noshie's breath away. "But how would we do it?" she gasped. "We haven't any human clothes."

"We'll sneak into the jumble room at the village hall," said Skirty Marm excitedly, "where they keep all the things that don't sell at jumble sales."

"But what about my green skin?"

Skirty Marm had forgotten about this, but thought quickly. "We'll borrow some face paint from the Drama Club," she said. "I'm sure I saw a stick of white in their cupboard. We could say you're pale with happiness. And I'll say my skin's gone grey because of too much joy!"

Old Noshie had caught on at last and she was beaming like a lighthouse. "We wouldn't even be breaking our promise to Mr B.," she said. "Because we only promised we wouldn't let Alice see two witches. She won't even notice two more old ladies!"

Skirty Marm peeped out of the big belfry window. She had to make sure the coast was clear, since the whole village had been sworn to secrecy about the local magic. To the witches' annoyance, everyone had agreed that coming face to face with it on her first visit might put poor Alice off marrying their curate. They all remembered how shocked they'd been at first themselves.

The village street was deserted. So was the vicarage. Mr Babbercorn and Mr Snelling had driven off in the vicar's car to meet Alice at the station. Mendax was sulking in the garden shed. Not a soul saw Old Noshie and Skirty Marm fluttering down from the church belfry to the village hall on their broomsticks.

The Power Hat was hidden underneath the new extension to the hall, but there was no time to worry about it now. Skirty Marm absent-mindedly checked the gigantic hollyhocks outside the hall and pulled out a dandelion that had grown to the size of a cabbage.

While Old Noshie ate the dandelion (she never could resist a juicy weed), Skirty Marm mumbled a quick spell to open the window of the jumble room. It was high up, and rather small, but Skirty Marm was a nimble witch and she scrambled up easily. Old Noshie, twice as plump and not nearly so nimble, had to be pulled up by her friend.

When they were both safely inside the small airless jumble room, the two witches gazed around in wonder. It was crammed from floor to ceiling with heaps of jumble – bags of clothes, boxes of dusty old books, battered bits of furniture.

"*Wow!*" cried Old Noshie. "Look at all this treasure!" She picked up a picture, in a broken frame, of some white horses running on a beach. "Why would anyone give a beautiful thing like this to a jumble sale? It would look very elegant in our belfry."

Skirty Marm had found a large shopping bag made of bright pink plastic. "Very tasteful," she remarked. "I'll use this to carry my witch-clothes. I'd hate my best rags to get sold at a jumble sale by mistake."

"We'll bring it all back," Old Noshie said, "so it won't be like stealing. Except the picture. Don't these horses look real? You can almost taste them!"

Skirty Marm wasn't listening. She had just found something amazing and extraordinary in the pink bag. "Nosh – look!"

Like a conjuror pulling a rabbit from a hat, she drew from the bag a large brown bottle of Nasty Medicine.

Now, as every human being ought to know, drinking someone else's Nasty Medicine is a very STUPID and DANGEROUS thing to do – practically as bad as taking POISON. Witches are not humans, however, and on Witch Island, Nasty Medicine is considered a great treat. All it does to witches is to make them disgracefully tipsy.

In the past, this revolting drink had got Old

Noshie and Skirty Marm into terrible trouble. You could say that it had been their downfall, since it was Nasty Medicine that had inspired them to sing the rude song about Mrs Abercrombie. You'd think they would have seen enough of it – they had sworn to Mr Babbercorn that they would never touch another drop – but both witches stared at the brown bottle with greedy longing.

"We can't just leave it in the bag, can we?" Old Noshie asked hopefully.

Skirty Marm was stern. "Certainly *not*! Putting it back in that bag would be terribly careless of us. What if some poor human drank it? No, Noshie. It is our DUTY to drink this Nasty Medicine AT ONCE, before it falls into the wrong hands."

"I quite agree!" cried Old Noshie.

Skirty took the top off the bottle. "I don't want to get you into trouble, Nosh – so I'll drink it."

"OH, NO YOU DON'T!" roared Old Noshie. "Gimme my share, you thieving old weasel, or I'll squash your nose!"

She slapped Skirty Marm. Skirty Marm slapped Old Noshie. An unseemly scuffle broke out, during which Old Noshie rammed Skirty Marm's head into an old suitcase, and Skirty Marm threw Old Noshie's blue wig out of the window.

Finally, they settled the argument by making a fingermark on the label of the bottle and drinking exactly half each. The Nasty Medicine was out of date (which made it even more dangerous to humans) and smelt so incredibly disgusting that no human would have touched it anyway.

"DEE-LICIOUS!" cried Skirty Marm.

"YUM-YUM!" cried Old Noshie.

And as drunken witches do, they began to sing a vulgar song.

"Medicine Molly is my name –
Medicine-guzzling is my game!
There's no other drink like ME-DI-CINE –
It makes you giggle and it makes you grin!

All round the island it's the same –
For ME-DI-CINE I got my name!
Excuse me while I lie down in the gutter –
Medicine Molly is my name!"

Then (as drunken witches do) they cried a little and swore eternal friendship. Neither was at all ashamed of her disgraceful and appalling behaviour.

Nasty Medicine always made Skirty Marm feel very brave and clever. "Now for our costumes!" she cried. "Do what I do, Nosh – remember, we have to talk like the other Old Folk at the Drop-In Club. It couldn't be easier."

Old Noshie hiccuped loudly. "Lucky Alice – now she's going to meet the most interesting old ladies in Tranters End!"

*

By tea time, Mr Babbercorn was feeling a little anxious. Alice had arrived safely at the vicarage, and the lunch with the churchwardens had been a splendid success. Mendax had kept well out of sight – except once, when he was seen chasing a bird across the lawn.

Alice had said, "What a sweet cat!"

All in all, everything was going beautifully. But Mr Babbercorn had expected to see the faces of the witches at the top of the church tower, peeping out of the belfry window – and there had been no sign of them.

"I don't like it," he whispered anxiously to the vicar. "They're up to something."

Mr Snelling was enjoying all the food and festivity. "Nonsense!" he said happily. "Noshie and Skirty are never naughty these days. You haven't seen them because they're being extra-good – I'm proud of them!"

"Hmmm," said Mr Babbercorn doubtfully. "I hope you're right."

The members of the Old Folks' Drop-In Club were walking up to the vicarage front door for their tea party. All the old ladies were wearing their best hats, and all the old gentlemen had flowers in their buttonholes. Mrs Miller, who played the piano at their sing-songs and liked to say she was "EIGHTY-THREE YEARS YOUNG", was carrying a large bunch of flowers for Alice.

Despite his worries about the witches, Mr Babbercorn felt very proud. Alice looks so pretty in her blue dress, he thought. She was passing around plates of cakes and shouting at deaf Miss Venables as if she'd lived in Tranters End all her life.

"That girl will be a blessing on the village," Mrs Miller told him. "I'm sure she'll soon get used to – to *you-know-who*."

Mrs Miller was a special friend of the witches who had introduced them to the Old Folks' Drop-In Club. She had invited them to tea in her cottage and told them to call her "Doris".

"Don't you fret, dear," she reassured the curate. "It couldn't be going better!"

At this moment, the doorbell rang again.

"That's funny," said Mr Snelling. "We're not expecting anyone else."

Mrs Miller went to answer the door. She came back into the sitting room a moment later with a very strange expression on her face.

"Something the matter, Doris?" asked Mr Snelling.

"N-n-no," Mrs Miller said doubtfully. "It's just that . . . er . . . two more members of our club have popped in unexpectedly."

"That's nice," said Alice, smiling.

Mr Babbercorn choked on a brandy snap. He knew exactly who these unexpected old folk would be, and it was too late to do anything about it.

To the horror of everyone except Alice, two very peculiar old ladies came shuffling into the room. One held a large pink shopping bag, stuffed with something dark. The other clutched a dusty picture.

"Well, dear. You must be Alice," said Skirty Marm in her best imitation of Mrs Miller. She shook Alice's hand. "Welcome to Tranters End, dear. My name is Miss Skirt, and this is my friend, Miss Nosh."

"Rubbish!" said Old Noshie loudly.

Skirty Marm hissed, "What are you talking about?"

Old Noshie hiccuped defiantly. "My name's not Miss Nosh – that's just stupid! I'm a dear old soul called Mrs Worksnap."

"How do you do," said Alice politely.

"I'm afraid Miss Nosh is a terrible old fool, dear," Skirty Marm said sternly. "Take no notice of her. I've no idea where she got this 'Worksnap' business."

Mr Babbercorn tugged at the vicar's sleeve. "This is *ghastly*!" he whispered frantically. "Heaven knows where they found it, but I'd swear those two have been at the Nasty Medicine – they stink of it! We've got to get rid of them!"

Alice was a very polite young woman, but she couldn't help staring. Both these strange old ladies wore knitted hats, pulled down low over their foreheads – Miss Skirt's hat seemed to be a tea cosy. The face of Miss Nosh (or "Mrs Worksnap") was covered in thick white paint. The backs of her ears appeared to be bright green. The face of Miss Skirt was an unhealthy shade of grey, and her eyes were hidden behind a pair of sunglasses. Although the weather was warm, both Miss Nosh and Miss Skirt were wrapped in thick brown coats and wore lumpy brown stockings.

"Do have a scone," said Alice, holding out a plate to the two witchy ladies.

"YUM!" shouted Old Noshie.

Skirty Marm nudged her, to remind her that they were supposed to be behaving like senior humans.

"I don't mind if I do, dear," Skirty Marm said, in her best Mrs Miller voice.

Alice glanced curiously around the room. Everyone – except Miss Nosh and Miss Skirt – had gone very quiet. Mr Babbercorn was as pale as his own white collar. Mr Snelling had begun to hum (as he always did when he was feeling nervous).

"Do sit down," Alice said kindly to the two old ladies.

"I'm afraid you'll have to SPEAK UP, dear," Skirty Marm said. She was starting to enjoy being a real old lady. "I left my hearing aid on the draining board."

This had once happened to a gentleman in the club called Mr Fisher, who now startled Alice by giving a sudden snort of laughter.

Skirty Marm plumped down on the sofa, pulling Old Noshie down beside her. There was a long uneasy silence.

Alice asked politely, "Have you lived here long?"

"AGES!" cried Skirty Marm.

"You must be full of wonderful stories about the village."

"COR, THAT'S PUTTING IT MILDLY!" shouted Miss Nosh.

Miss Skirt scowled and nudged her friend very hard.

"You'll have to excuse Miss Nosh, dear. She only sounds barmy because she's been drinking."

Mr Babbercorn let out a strangled yelp. Mr Snelling choked on a spoonful of trifle, spraying jelly far and wide. Mrs Miller and Mr Fisher were struggling not to giggle.

"We're a marvellous old pair," Skirty Marm went on. "Got all our marbles."

"Oh, I'm sure," said Alice.

"I always say, I'm A HUNDRED AND FIFTY-THREE YEARS YOUNG!"

"Goodness," said Alice. "What a tremendous age!"

"And I feel the cold," said Skirty Marm. "Even in summer, I never go out without two thick pairs of bloomers. Want to see them?"

Mr Babbercorn could bear no more. He leapt to the sofa and grabbed each witch by their bony hands.

"I'm afraid Miss Nosh and Miss Skirt have to leave now," he said firmly.

"No we don't," protested Old Noshie. "We haven't had any trifle."

"Yes, you do," said Mr Snelling, wiping jelly off his face with a tissue. "You have to leave *right now*."

Mr Babbercorn looked so angry that the dear old souls on the sofa sobered up at once. Even Miss Skirt realized, with a sinking heart, that the two most interesting old ladies in Tranters End were in very hot water indeed.

3

Dear Old Souls in Trouble

The telling-off took place in the belfry, early the next morning. Mr Babbercorn lectured Old Noshie and Skirty Marm for over an hour, but here is a brief summary of the points he covered.

1. He had never been so embarrassed in his life. Especially by:

   a) The ridiculous disguises worn by the witches.

   b) Skirty Marm's public mention of "bloomers" at a vicarage tea party.

   c) The obvious reek of Nasty Medicine.

2. Alice now thought she was coming to a village full of completely mad old ladies.

3. The witches had broken two major promises:

   a) That they would keep away from Alice, and

   b) that they would never touch another drop of Nasty Medicine.

33

4. Thanks to the awful behaviour of the witches, it would now be even more difficult for Mr Babbercorn to tell Alice about the magic at Tranters End.

Old Noshie and Skirty Marm listened in silence, looking very sulky and feeling terrible – they had both woken up with thumping headaches.

If Mr Babbercorn was looking for signs of remorse, however, he was disappointed. Neither witch was sorry. They were still furious with the curate for bundling them out of the vicarage tea party so rudely. Afterwards, they had flown up to the roof and shouted "BUM!" down the chimney.

"How could you do it?" cried Mr Babbercorn. "You knew how important it was for Alice to get a good impression!"

Skirty Marm scowled. "If you didn't like our disguises, you should have invited us to the party as *ourselves*. It's all your fault because you tried to hide us."

"YES!" shouted Old Noshie. She was not as clever with words as Skirty Marm, but she supported her friend by shouting "YES!" every few minutes.

"All you had to do was wait." Mr Babbercorn groaned. "I was going to introduce you to Alice at the right moment!"

His thin cheeks reddened as he said this. He knew it was the weakest part of his argument. Deep down, in his heart of hearts, he did rather wish that Alice didn't have to know about the witches. They thought he was ashamed of them, and he couldn't really deny it. Alice was the sweetest girl in the world, but what if she was shocked when she found out about the witches – and refused to marry him?

He sighed. "Witches, listen – I was cross yesterday, but Alice was very nice about it. Especially when I told her that Miss Nosh and Miss Skirt were leaving the village immediately."

"*Leaving?*" Skirty Marm was suspicious.

"Yes, and Alice is coming to stay in Tranters End." Mr Babbercorn hurried on, rather guiltily. "She's going to rent the spare room at Mrs Miller's cottage. Now, witches, I beg you – keep out of her way until I've explained about the magic!"

"Oh, *we'll* stay out of the way all right," said Skirty Marm with a dangerous glint in her eye.

("YES!" shouted Old Noshie.)

"Thank you," said Mr Babbercorn.

Skirty Marm smirked scornfully. "But I can't answer for Miss Nosh and Miss Skirt. Until you've explained to Alice, you're going to see a lot of those two!"

The poor young curate trudged down the one hundred and eighty-six belfry steps, feeling very worried and very sad. He knew he had deeply offended the witches by not introducing them to Alice straight away. And now they wanted to punish him. His spirits sank as he prepared himself for the difficult days ahead.

To Mr Babbercorn's dismay, Miss Nosh and Miss Skirt were waiting – wearing their ridiculous costumes – outside Mrs Miller's cottage on the day Alice moved in.

"Dear old souls," said Alice. "I thought you said they'd left."

"They've come back," Mr Babbercorn said gloomily.

"They seem very kind," Alice said, "but ever so odd. Miss Skirt can't really be a hundred and fifty-three! And why does Miss Nosh plaster herself in that white stuff?"

"It's ointment," lied the curate miserably.

"She suffers from a rare skin disease."

"Poor old thing," sighed Alice. "Well, I'll look forward to seeing a lot of them, now I'm here."

And see a lot of them she certainly did. For the next two weeks, every time Mr Babbercorn tried to be alone with the woman he loved, out would pop Miss Nosh and Miss Skirt. They haunted Alice like a pair of barmy old ghosts.

When Alice and Mr Babbercorn went for a romantic stroll beside the river, there were Miss Nosh and Miss Skirt – sitting on the bank with their tongues sticking out.

"Why are they doing that?" wondered Alice.

"They're catching flies," said Mr Babbercorn, wincing as Old Noshie gulped down a dragonfly. "Ignore them."

Alice giggled. "It's like that song about the old woman who swallowed a fly. I didn't think it happened in real life!"

The vicarage garden was full of roses and extremely pretty. When Mr Babbercorn tried sitting there with Alice, however, he quickly noticed two beady pairs of eyes, and two pointed noses sticking through the trellis.

"Shouldn't we invite them in?" asked Alice.

"No," Mr Babbercorn said loudly.

He was beginning to be very annoyed with Old Noshie and Skirty Marm. The more they haunted Alice, the more determined he was not to tell her a thing until they stopped behaving so rudely.

In church, during the hymn "Guide Me, O Thou Great Redeemer", the witches sang "Tell Her, O Thou Stinky Curate!"

Skirty Marm, in particular, was at least as determined as Mr Babbercorn.

The curate was a gentle and kind-hearted man, but his patience was being stretched to its limit. It snapped one warm evening when he took Alice for a walk in the woods.

Just as he was murmuring, "Isn't this peaceful?", there was a sound of snapping wood, and Old Noshie crashed down from a tree on to the path in front of them.

"Good gracious," said Alice. "Are you hurt, Miss Nosh?" Polite as she was, she couldn't help looking astonished. She had never met any very old ladies who climbed trees.

"I told her that branch was rotten," said Skirty Marm's voice from above them.

Old Noshie stood up, rubbing her bottom. "I wanted to get a good view!"

"Miss Skirt," said Mr Babbercorn sternly, "kindly come down from that tree."

"NO!" shouted Skirty Marm. "I WON'T!"

"Excuse me, Alice," Mr Babbercorn said, through gritted teeth. "Would you mind walking back to Mrs Miller's by yourself? I have some urgent business to settle, with Old . . . I mean, with Miss Nosh and Miss Skirt."

"Of course I don't mind," said Alice, secretly wondering why her future husband looked so cross. "Good evening, ladies."

As soon as she'd gone, the curate snapped, "Skirty Marm – DOWN!"

And his voice was so strict that Skirty Marm scrambled down from her tree at once.

"This," said Mr Babbercorn, "has got to stop!"

Skirty Marm stuck out her lip stubbornly. "It'll stop when you tell Alice we're really witches."

"I'm not saying a word to her," said Mr Babbercorn, "until I've gone at least two weeks without seeing Miss Nosh and Miss Skirt."

"Two weeks!" wailed Old Noshie."We can't hide for two whole weeks!"

"Alice will wonder what's happened to the

dear old ladies," Skirty Marm pointed out smugly.

"I'll say they've both been killed in a freak accident!" shouted Mr Babbercorn, losing his temper at last. "Because if this persecution goes on for much longer it won't be far from the truth! I've a good mind to stuff the pair of you into a wheelie bin and pay the dustmen to take you away! Witches, you have got to leave us alone!"

With this, Mr Babbercorn stomped angrily away through the woods – the mild young curate, who had never stomped in his life.

There was a moment of silence while the witches stared after him, their mouths gaping with surprise.

Old Noshie burst into tears. "Oh, Skirt! What have we done? We were MEAN to our friend – and now he doesn't want to see us EVER AGAIN!"

"Huh! I don't care!" said Skirty Marm.

But she didn't sound very sure. For the truth was, she *did* care – very much indeed. Life without Mr Babbercorn would be as dull and flavourless as bat pudding without treacle.

4

Emergency

Old Noshie was still crying when the witches went to bed that night. Her tears had washed away her "Miss Nosh" face paint, so that her woebegone cheeks were striped green and white.

Skirty Marm was still putting up a great show of not caring, but finding it harder and harder to hide her misery. This was the worst quarrel they'd ever had with their best friend.

The misery of the witches didn't last long, however. In the middle of the night, when the moon rode high above St Tranter's Church, the witches were woken by a loud hammering on the belfry door.

It was Mr Babbercorn, and he looked dreadful – pale as a ghost, with all his hair standing on end. He was gasping for breath because he had just pelted like lightning up the one hundred and eighty-six steps.

"Witches, you've got to forgive me – I need your help!"

Old Noshie and Skirty Marm understood at once that Something Terrible had happened. Skirty Marm fetched the curate her cushion (there were no chairs in the belfry), and Old Noshie put the kettle on (which is always a good thing to do in an emergency).

When he'd got his breath back, Mr Babbercorn gasped, "It's Alice – she's VANISHED!"

Old Noshie cried, "Oh, no! She's run away because we were naughty!" And she was all set to burst into tears again.

"Shut up, fusspot," said Skirty Marm, not unkindly. "Alice wouldn't just run away, would she, Mr B.?"

"*Never!*" Mr Babbercorn said firmly. "Alice would never go anywhere without telling me. But witches, I can't ask you for help until I've apologized. I admit that I wasn't as proud as I should have been to have the two of you as my friends. I should have introduced you to Alice straight away. I'm not asking you to help for my sake, but if you care at all about Alice—"

He broke off, and a tear rolled down his pale cheek.

43

Old Noshie and Skirty Marm were deeply touched by this noble apology.

"We're sorry too," said Skirty Marm. "We know it was very cheeky to spy on you – don't we, Nosh?"

"We'll *never* do it again!" Old Noshie wiped her nose on her sleeve, leaving a smear of white face paint.

Mr Babbercorn wiped his nose on a proper handkerchief. "Dear witches, it's all forgotten now. Alice has vanished, and you are the only people in the world I can turn to!"

Old Noshie made them all a refreshing cup of warm rainwater with a spoonful of mud (witches hate human tea), and Mr Babbercorn told them the story of Alice's mysterious disappearance.

Nobody had seen her since she left the witches and Mr Babbercorn in the woods. She hadn't returned to Mrs Miller's cottage, and Mrs Miller had telephoned the vicarage two hours ago, very worried.

"The vicar and Mendax and I searched the woods for her, calling her name, but there was no sign of her." Mr Babbercorn sipped his rainwater without seeming to taste it, which was probably just as well. "We got home, and I was just about to ring PC Bloater when something fell down the chimney."

Turning a shade paler, Mr Babbercorn took the "something" out of his jacket pocket and gave it to Skirty Marm. It was a thick piece of paper, smeared with soot and dirt. On it was scrawled in blotted brown ink:

"IF YOU WANT ALICE GIVE ME
THE HAT!"

"AAARGH!" screamed Old Noshie, dropping her cup. "It's the queen! The queen's stolen Alice!"

"Pull yourself together!" ordered Skirty Marm. "This is no time to panic!"

"YES IT IS!" Old Noshie wailed.

Skirty Marm turned to Mr Babbercorn. "This note is definitely from Mrs Abercrombie, Queen of the Witches."

Mr Babbercorn nodded sadly. "That's what Mendax said. He said it was no use calling PC Bloater. He said Mrs Abercrombie would *stop at nothing* to get her hands on that Power Hat."

"But how did Mrs A. do it?" cried Old Noshie. "She doesn't have the power to go around kidnapping humans!"

Skirty Marm was gloomy. "Don't you remember anything from school, you daft old brush? A witch can always kidnap a human if she wants to. Alice must have left a loophole."

"A loophole?" Mr Babbercorn was bewildered.

"It's when a human does something that allows magic in," Skirty Marm explained. "Maybe Alice trod on hemlock with her left foot, or walked round the church with her back to the sun, or forgot to kiss the first hare she saw by moonlight. Those things don't normally matter – unless a witch is watching you like a hawk, *waiting to pounce*."

Mr Babbercorn had never seen the ex-queen of the Witches, but he had heard enough about her to make him shudder now. The thought of the horrible old monster waiting to pounce on his Alice was awful.

"Where do you think Mrs Abercrombie has taken her?" he whispered desperately. "Can you bring her back?"

"We *have* to," said Skirty Marm, getting gloomier by the minute. "If we can't find Alice by ourselves, we'll have to give Mrs A. the Power Hat. And if we give her the Hat—"

"She'll KILL us!" Old Noshie finished for her.

"I won't allow you to give up the Hat," Mr Babbercorn said bravely. "I know Alice would say the same. But – can anything be done?" His eyes were pleading, and so were Old Noshie's.

Skirty Marm was thinking so hard her purple hair crackled with electricity. She'd won the Spellbinder's Medal for thirty-six years in a row, but could she handle something as tough as this? Did she dare to fight a battle of wits with Mrs Abercrombie?

"There's the advanced finding spell," she said slowly. "I've only done it once. It's ever so tricky."

"I remember!" Old Noshie began to dance with excitement. "You used it to find my singing yo-yo when I dropped it in the sea! Don't worry, Mr B. – our chemistry teacher said Skirty was the best finder in the school!"

Skirty Marm was not at all sure she could remember the whole of this complicated spell, but she hated to disappoint the poor curate.

"We'll give it a try," she declared, doing her best to sound very confident. "Nosh, nip outside and catch me an old pigeon – one with plenty of mites."

"Righty-ho!" shouted Old Noshie. She grabbed her broomstick and jumped out of the belfry window – a sight that always made Mr Babbercorn dizzy. He watched as Skirty Marm picked up her pointed hat and started to fill it with various strange ingredients.

"Let me see . . . dried slugs, powdered frogspawn – drat, we're nearly out of beetle's elbows—"

Old Noshie crashed back into the belfry, clutching an ancient smelly pigeon. "Have we got everything, Skirt?"

"We need some salt, some bicarbonate of soda and a bar of soap." Skirty Marm was frowning with the effort of recalling the spell. "We'd better go down to the vicarage."

Mr Babbercorn jumped up eagerly, glad to be doing something. Old Noshie stuffed the cross old pigeon into her hat, jammed it on her head and picked up the iron cauldron they had got mail-order from Witch Island. It was very heavy, but witches are stronger than humans and she carried it as easily as a sack of feathers. The three of them ran down the one hundred and eighty-six belfry steps and out into the warm summer night.

The houses along the village street were dark, but the windows of the vicarage blazed with light. In the kitchen they found Mendax, and the vicar in his dressing gown. Mr Snelling sprang out of his chair the moment he saw the witches.

"Thank heavens! You've got to find poor Alice!"

His eyes grew round with amazement as Skirty Marm unpacked her hatful of ingredients onto the kitchen table.

Mendax stood on his hind legs and tied on his apron. "Let me help. I've assisted at a finding spell before – and I'm not lying," he added quickly. "I never lie in an emergency. It was when Mrs Wilkins lost her keys in the Main Sewer." (Mrs Wilkins was the nasty drunken old Purple-Stocking who had once owned the little black cat on Witch Island.) "I'll mash the dried slugs in milk," offered Mendax, "if someone else will drop in the pigeon mites."

"Drat, I forgot about that bird," said Old Noshie. "The mites'll be crawling all over my wig by now!" She took the pigeon out of her hat.

"YEUCH!" exclaimed the vicar. "What a revolting bird – it's got things living in its feathers!"

Mendax lit a candle and poured milk into his small, cat-sized saucepan.

"Mr Snelling," he mewed, "get your tweezers. Pick out the mites and drop them in while I stir."

"Oh, yes – anything!" Mr Snelling dashed to the bathroom for his tweezers, tripping over the cord of his dressing gown in his excitement.

"Mr B.," Skirty Marm said, "go into the garden and fetch me six blades of grass, a fresh caterpillar and a dandelion root."

Mr Babbercorn snatched up his torch and rushed out into the dark garden. Mendax stirred his saucepan above the candle flame. Old Noshie lit the gas under the cauldron. Soon, the vicarage kitchen had been transformed into a sorcerer's cave. The vicar and the curate, who did not normally approve of magic, followed Skirty Marm's instructions like a pair of sorcerer's apprentices.

Mr Snelling picked mites off the revolting old pigeon with his tweezers and dropped them one by one into Mendax's saucepan. Mr Babbercorn (sniffing to himself, because he was so worried about Alice) peeled and grated the dandelion root. Old Noshie and Skirty Marm muttered spells and stirred the bubbling cauldron – which looked very strange indeed, sitting on the vicarage stove.

"Pooh! What a pong!" complained Mr Snelling. "Do all spells smell as nasty as this?"

"Nasty?" Old Noshie was surprised. She thought the smell was delicious.

The kitchen was filling with dark blue smoke. Mendax added his saucepan of brownish gloop to the cauldron. As the little black cat moved, the pigeon shrieked and fluttered away out of the open back door.

"Huh! As if I'd eat an old fleabag like him," Mendax muttered scornfully. "I may be a cat, but I'm not *that* desperate."

Finally, the mixture was ready.

Skirty Marm bent over the cauldron and murmured the finding spell, praying she had remembered it correctly.

"Don't worry," Old Noshie whispered kindly to Mr Babbercorn. "We made it extra strong."

A loud rumble, rather like a huge burp, shook the cauldron.

"Here it comes!" shouted Skirty Marm.

Suddenly, to the astonishment of the vicar and the curate, the kitchen was jammed with things that had been lost. There were hundreds of coins from between the sofa cushions of every house in the village (when the vicar counted the money later it came to £246.83, which he gave to Oxfam). There were sixteen umbrellas, thirty-eight odd socks, two pairs of false teeth and Mr Fisher's pension book. Everything in Tranters End that had been lost was now found.

Except Alice.

There was a long silence.

Mr Babbercorn collapsed into a chair. "It didn't work!" he groaned.

"Excuse me," Skirty Marm was offended. "It worked perfectly!"

"Of course, of course," Mr Snelling said kindly. "Poor Cuthbert is simply worried about poor dear Alice. What on earth do we do now?"

"Nothing," said Old Noshie in a trembling voice. "If the advanced finding spell can't find her, it means she can't be found."

Yet again, she began to cry. It was terrible to think of Alice in the clutches of Mrs Abercrombie. Skirty Marm's lips wobbled. The vicar and the curate blew their noses. Mendax wiped his green eyes on his tail.

"Thanks, witches," Mr Babbercorn said quietly. "You did your best."

"Well, it's been nice knowing you all," gulped Old Noshie. "Me and Skirt will be dead quite soon, because we've got to tell Mrs A. where we hid the Power Hat, or we'll never see Alice again."

"*No!*" cried Mr Babbercorn. "I can't let you do it! There must be something else we can try!"

"Wait a minute!" Skirty Marm gave such a leap of excitement that her head banged against the ceiling. "What an *idiot* I am! Why didn't I think of it before? Never mind how strong Mrs A.'s spell is – our magic is even stronger, because WE'VE GOT THE HAT!"

She looked round at their gaping puzzled faces and stamped her foot impatiently. "Don't you see? The Power Hat can find anything in the whole world!"

"But . . . but . . . but . . ." stammered Old Noshie, "we buried the Hat!"

"Then we have to UN-bury it!" yelled Skirty Marm. "Come on!"

There was not a second to lose. Mr Snelling (still in his dressing gown and slippers) fetched four spades – and a small trowel for Mendax – from the garden shed. Quietly and fearfully, not knowing who might be watching, they crept through the dark village to the hall.

"Crikey," whispered the vicar, "look at the size of those hollyhocks! Why on earth couldn't old Mrs Whatsit spot where you'd buried the Hat?"

"Because without the Hat on her head she doesn't have enough power," said Skirty Marm. "Her tracking system just isn't sophisticated enough. Noshie, Mendax and I are protected by magical force fields which she can't penetrate at long-range," she explained. "So she must have operated some kind of advanced retrieval spell to kidnap Alice. Even without the Hat, Mrs Abercrombie is a very clever witch."

"But how can *we* get at the Power Hat?" Mr Babbercorn cried despairingly. "It's right under the foundations of the new extension!"

The witches and Mendax exchanged uneasy glances.

Mendax said, "Now, Vicar – I hope you're not going to be difficult about this—"

Before the words were out of his mouth, there was a blinding flash of light. The vicar and the curate were blown right off their feet into the shrubbery. Lumps of earth, brick and cement rained down on their heads.

When Mr Babbercorn had wiped the dust off his glasses, he gasped with horror. One side of the village hall lay in ruins. All that was left of the new extension was a heap of smoking rubble.

"Sorry about that," said Skirty Marm.

"My lovely extension!" moaned Mr Snelling. "Have you any idea how many jumble sales it took to raise the money for that?"

Mendax daintily spat out crumbs of plaster. "Do stop fussing, Vicar. Alice is worth a thousand extensions."

Skirty Marm looked into the large crater made by her magical explosion. The everlasting candle at the point of the Power Hat was poking out of the heap of debris, bathing everything in its eerie silver light. All the friends climbed down into the hole and quickly dug out the rest of the Hat.

"I don't know how I'm going to explain this to the churchwardens," puffed Mr Snelling, digging furiously. "And where are the choir supposed to practise now?"

The Power Hat had been buried under several metres of concrete. When the witches carefully brushed off the last bits of rubble, however, it was black, gleaming and perfect, without so much as a smudge or a dent. They pulled it out of the hole and placed it solemnly on the ground. It was taller than any of them.

Old Noshie shivered. "I don't like it. I've never liked that Hat."

Mendax said nothing, but jumped nervously into the vicar's dressing-gown pocket.

"Here goes," said Skirty Marm. She handed her own black pointed hat to Old Noshie and put on the Power Hat. She'd worn it before, while bringing it back from Witch Island, so she was prepared for the strange, buzzing, crowded feeling it gave the wearer's brain.

She closed her eyes and whispered, "Find Alice Wisk."

As she felt the might of the Power Hat surrounding her, Skirty Marm realized that Mrs Abercrombie had hidden Alice behind many layers of strong magic. She heard the Hat slicing through them, one by one. Then, inside her head, she saw green letters appearing – rather like the letters on an old-fashioned computer screen.

"*Alice is in the woods*," she read aloud, "*at the north end of the bridge.*"

"But we've already looked for her there!" cried Mr Babbercorn. "I called and called her name!"

"The Power Hat is never wrong," said Mendax, popping his head out of the vicar's pocket. "Get a move on, Mr Snelling. We haven't a second to lose!"

The woods were pitch-dark. Mr Snelling and Mr Babbercorn switched on their torches, and the witches lit the ends of their fingers (this is not painful for witches). But they were all disappointed to reach the north end of the small wooden bridge and find no Alice.

Skirty Marm closed her eyes again. "You stupid old Hat – where's Alice?"

And again, the green letters appeared inside her head. "*None of your cheek!*" she read. "*Why don't you look properly? Third dock leaf from the big stone.*"

Skirty Marm didn't have time to be annoyed by the Hat's lofty tone. Torches and lighted fingers were instantly trained on the tangle of weeds beside the river.

"Well, I can't see a sausage," Old Noshie said crossly. "There's nothing here but a lot of *snails*."

The snails were oozing about under a row of dock leaves, groping blindly with their tiny horns.

"Just a minute," muttered Mendax. He jumped out of the vicar's pocket and disappeared among the weeds. A moment later, the others heard a long loud "Miaow!" of amazement and knew things must be serious – usually, the elegant cat thought miaowing rather vulgar. He came out of the weeds on his hind legs, carrying something very carefully between his front paws. It was a snail with a brown shell, a little larger than the others.

In the night silence of the woods, there was a very very quiet squeak, which sounded very much like "*Help*".

Mr Babbercorn shone his torch directly at the snail. If you squinted very closely, you could see a tiny face just under its horns. And that face had a definite look of . . .

"ALICE!" choked Mr Babbercorn.

5

The Professor

Naturally, Skirty Marm shut her eyes at once.

"Power Hat!" she shouted joyfully. "Let this snail be changed back into Alice Wisk!"

She waited for the green letters to appear inside her head. The waiting stretched into minutes. Skirty Marm saw nothing, except darkness.

"Come on!" she growled.

At last, the letters appeared. "*Search completed*," Skirty Marm read aloud. "*The metamorphic reach is outside my circle.*"

"Blimey," muttered Old Noshie. "What's that in Hinglish?"

Mr Babbercorn had turned so pale that his lips were grey.

"I think . . ." he choked. "I think the Hat is saying it can't help Alice."

The mouths of the witches dropped open in

amazement.

"But it *must* help her!" cried Mr Snelling. "You said it could do anything!"

Skirty Marm shut her eyes again. "Now look here, Hat – what's going on?"

The Hat typed, and she read, "*The human male in the collar is correct. The spell has been locked – by a locking charm from behind the Hills of Time. This is beyond my power. I can do nothing.*"

"NOTHING!" shouted Old Noshie. "Call yourself a Power Hat? We've been cheated!"

"What on earth are we going to do?" the vicar wondered miserably. "You can't have a wedding when the bride's a snail!"

"We won't give up," said Mr Babbercorn. "Be brave, Alice – we'll think of something!" And he took his snail-bride from Mendax and gently kissed her shell.

"It all happened in a flash," Alice squeaked in her tiny snail's voice. "One minute I was walking through the woods on two legs. The next minute I was sliding along on my stomach, leaving a disgusting trail of slime."

"Oh, please don't worry about your slime

trail," the vicar said kindly. "I think it's rather pretty."

"This has all been such a surprise," said Alice. "First being turned into a snail – and then finding the vicarage full of witches and talking cats. I keep thinking I must be dreaming!"

Mr Snelling sighed. "I wish you were!"

The snail that was Alice lay in a saucer on top of the kitchen table. Her friends sat around her, drinking cups of hot chocolate made by Mendax. They had explained the whole situation to the bewildered mollusc and were now trying to look cheerful.

"You're not to worry about anything," Mr

Babbercorn told Alice. "You can sleep quite comfortably in the old fish tank, and you must tell me which leaves you like best."

"Sorry I eat such an awful lot," squeaked the tiny voice. "I can't seem to help it. Those mulberry leaves were very tasty."

"I picked those," Old Noshie said proudly. "Is there anything else you fancy?"

"Well," Alice said, "now that you mention it, I can't stop thinking about thick cardboard."

"Ah, the brown sort," said Skirty Marm knowingly. "Yes, it is rather delicious."

While Alice was looking at Skirty Marm, Mr Babbercorn quickly wiped away two tears. He was doing his best to be cheerful for Alice's sake, but he felt that his dreams were in ruins. The poor young man was now imagining the writing on his tombstone:

"Cuthbert Babbercorn, Late Curate of this
   Parish,
Died of Grief when his Beloved was
   Transformed.
Also Alice, Snail of the Above."

The vicar's kind heart ached for his curate. "I wish I understood all that rigmarole about the

Hills of Time," he sighed. "What have they got to do with the Power Hat not being able to change Alice back?"

"We did it at school," Skirty Marm said. "The Hills of Time are where time began. The locking charm must have come from the Gardens Before Time."

"It all sounds very complicated," said Mr Snelling crossly.

Mendax put a pawful of mulberry leaves in front of Alice.

"Goodness knows how Mrs Abercrombie got her hands on such a valuable antique spell," he remarked. "She must have paid a fortune for it on the black market."

"You've lost me," complained the vicar. "Is there such a thing as an antique spell – like an antique chair or an old painting?"

"The Witch Island Museum is full of them," Mendax said. "Beautiful old spells, with gorgeous decorations." A faraway look came into his green eyes. "When I was a kitten, I often drew inspiration from those priceless works of art. As a matter of fact, I saw a very famous locking charm once – the Stumpenberg Trivet, as it is popularly known."

Old Noshie rudely blew a raspberry. "You LIAR! You've never seen the Stumpenberg Trivet! It's kept hidden away in case someone nicks it!"

Mendax was offended. "I didn't say I'd seen it in real life. I had a picture of it, on a calendar."

Skirty Marm scowled. "I bet Mrs Abercrombie used something like it, though. She wanted to make sure we could never reverse the spell unless we gave her that wretched Hat! Oh, I wish I'd never taken it!"

Mr Babbercorn's white face was thoughtful. "When we humans have something very old and precious, lots of scholars write about it. We put everything they write in libraries. Is there a library on Witch Island?"

Skirty Marm leapt to her feet. "Of course! The State Library! Nosh – we have to get in touch with Professor Mouldypage!"

"Don't be silly!" cried Old Noshie. "You wouldn't *dare*! And anyway, how would you find her? It's like a human trying to telephone the prime minister – impossible!"

Professor Mouldypage was in charge of the Witch Island State Library. She was an ancient, mysterious witch – older than Mrs Abercrombie

– and such a brilliant scholar that even the ex-queen treated her with respect.

Mendax smoothed his ears smugly. "You forget, I am a *radio expert*. During the Battle of Fungus Gulch, when the enemy had us cornered, I was the only one who could get the message through to headquarters—"

"Mendax, please stop lying," interrupted Mr Snelling. "We all know perfectly well that you were nowhere near the Battle of Fungus Gulch. You weren't even born then."

"Well, perhaps I wasn't the *only* one who radioed HQ," Mendax said, in an icy mew. "I exaggerate sometimes, as old soldiers will. Let us proceed to the shed."

In his days as one of the queen's spies, Mendax had contacted Witch Island on a secret radio set, hidden inside the garden shed. He still used it, to listen to the witch football and chat to his cat friends.

Now he led everyone through the dark vicarage garden. Mr Snelling carried a large torch, and Mr Babbercorn held Alice, on her saucer.

"Please don't lose hope," he whispered to her. "We'll move mountains to free you if we have to! And I'll always love you, Alice – even if you stay a snail!"

The four of them, plus Alice and Mendax, were rather a tight fit in the shed. Mr Snelling took out the lawnmower so they could all crowd round the radio.

Mendax put on his cat-sized headphones. His neat paws pressed buttons and turned dials. "I'm afraid I'm going to have to tell a few small lies," he said, "or we'll never get through."

After a great many stupendous lies, he

managed to get through to the cave of Professor Mouldypage.

Her musty dusty voice came crackling out of the radio. "What is the meaning of this impertinence? Who *dares* to disturb me?"

Both gabbling nervously at the same time, the witches poured out the sad story of Alice, Mr Babbercorn and the kidnapping.

"So, you want to unlock the spell," croaked the professor. "Why should I help you? Keep the Power Hat and let the human woman remain a snail."

Both witches gasped with horror.

"We don't care about the Hat!" shouted Old Noshie. "Alice is MORE IMPORTANT!"

Over the radio came a loud snort of anger.

"A little human being, MORE IM-PORTANT than the mighty Power Hat? MORE IMPORTANT than the greatest symbol of our nationhood? I don't know what you young witches are coming to! In my day, you'd have *eaten* that curate of yours by now!"

Mr Babbercorn and Mr Snelling shuddered. To them, the rasping old voice sounded like all the wicked witches they had read about in fairy tales.

"In the land of the humans," Skirty Marm said, "people you love are more important than anything. If we can't turn that snail back into Alice, we'll have to give the Power Hat back to Mrs Abercrombie."

"And be killed in a horrible sort of way," Old Noshie couldn't help adding, "to be fixed on the morning of the execution, indoors if wet."

The professor's distant voice was full of amazement. "You care about the humans that much? You'd actually *die* for them?"

"Yes!" squeaked the witches, shaking in their ragged shoes.

"Well, burn my beard!" said Professor Mouldypage. To the witches' surprise, she chuckled. "I never liked Euphemia Abercrombie. Vulgar upstart – she was just the same at school. If you free your human without giving her the Hat, it'll serve THE OLD BAG RIGHT!" And she laughed her rusty laugh, like fingernails scratching a blackboard. "Heh, heh, heh!"

"Does that mean you'll help us?" gasped Mr Babbercorn.

"Yes, human," said the professor. "I do know a way. Don't imagine it will be easy. It might cost more than you are prepared to spend! To unlock the charm and reverse the spell, you need two berries from the Eert – that's the Backwards tree. It grows in the Gardens Before Time."

Skirty Marm groaned. She'd been hoping for a spell she could start right away. "But we don't know how to find the gardens!"

"Patience, young witch!" snapped the professor. "There is an entrance to the Gardens Before Time in the human world. If you find it and get through it, you'll earn your berries. Mrs Abercrombie has set you a trap, so don't take the Power Hat with you. Hide it somewhere safe."

"Our hiding place got blown up," Old Noshie said sadly.

"Into smithereens," added the Vicar.

"Then you must find a new one. And when you get the berries," the professor went on, "*if* you get them, perform a level six transforming spell backwards – leaving out the warts, and putting in the whole berries at the soft-boiled stage. Now, have you a pencil and paper? Put them down beside the radio."

Mr Snelling had a pencil in his pocket, and Old Noshie found a dusty paper bag. They watched as the pencil twitched, all by itself. Very quickly and neatly, it sketched out a map and marked one spot with an "X". The witches stared at it with round eyes – they were being shown one of the great secrets of the universe, beyond the reach of the Power Hat itself.

"Thanks, professor!" they chorused.

"This is very decent of you, Professor Mouldypage," said Mr Babbercorn. "Alice and I can't be grateful enough!"

"Oh, run along, run along!" shouted the professor, although she sounded quite pleased. "None of your *human mush*!"

The line went dead.

In the bright light of the vicarage kitchen, everyone stared at the map. It seemed to be a mass of straight lines and puzzling, squiggly writing.

"Londinium," read Old Noshie. "Where's that?"

"It's what the Romans used to call London," said Mr Snelling. "How fascinating! It must be a while since the professor visited the city."

"What's Pickydillo?" asked Mr Babbercorn anxiously. "And why has she written Cupid?"

The vicar smiled. "Another name for Cupid is Eros – it's the statue in the middle of Piccadilly Circus. So this long road must be Piccadilly."

He followed the road with his finger, and stopped at the cross. "Oh dear, this is rather inconvenient. It looks as if the entrance to the Gardens Before Time is right underneath my favourite shop!"

"Then that's where we'll go," declared Skirty Marm. "Give me the address."

"Oh, you can't miss it," said Mr Snelling smiling. "It's Fortnum and Mason's – one of the grandest and most famous food shops in the world!"

He coughed shyly. "I wonder, while you're there – could you pick up half a pound of chocolate almonds for me?"

6

A Visitor

There was no time to be lost. The witches began preparing for their journey to London the next morning. Mrs Miller – once she had got over the shock of Alice being a snail – was very helpful. To Mr Babbercorn's relief, she made some tactful suggestions about the outfits of "Miss Nosh" and "Miss Skirt". Old Noshie's face paint was changed from white to flesh colour, and Mrs Miller lent her a realistic brown wig to replace her blue one and cover her startlingly green bald head.

"I've nothing against green skin, dear," she said kindly, "but you have to look as much like proper humans as possible."

She lent Skirty Marm a real ladies' handbag made of shiny blue leather, and a more fashionable pair of sunglasses to hide her glittering red eyes. Both witches felt very elegant and stared at themselves in the mirror for ages.

"My hair looks like Alice's now," said Old Noshie. "I mean, like it did before she turned into a snail."

"Oh, *please* look after her!" begged Mr Babbercorn.

The vicar and the curate had an important meeting with the bishop that day, which they couldn't possibly miss. They weren't at all happy about sending the witches to London without them, but it couldn't be helped. Mendax and Alice were travelling with the witches, in a cat basket. Broomsticks would have attracted too much attention, so Mr Babbercorn had – reluctantly – decided they should go down on the train.

"Don't worry, Mr B.," said Skirty Marm cheerfully. They were all standing on the platform of the quiet country station, and Skirty Marm couldn't help looking forward to the adventure. "With any luck, you'll never see this snail again – because when we bring Alice back, she'll be a *person*."

"Do you remember all my instructions?" fussed Mr Snelling. "Is your money safe? And your packed lunch? Don't get the banknotes mixed up with the bat quiche – oh dear, why did that pesky bishop have to hold his meeting today?"

"No magic, unless it's to help Alice," Mr Babbercorn reminded them firmly. "No fighting, no jumping out of windows, no eating mice in public – are you *sure* you'll be all right?"

Old Noshie and Skirty Marm didn't reply. The London train was pulling into the station, and they had no eyes or ears for anything else. There are no railways on Witch Island, and the witches had never seen a train at close quarters. The size and speed of it amazed them. Once they were inside the train, the witches were deeply impressed by the bounciness of the seats.

Outside the window, the vicar and the curate carried on shouting advice, but the witches were too busy to listen. They were admiring their little table. Old Noshie immediately opened her packed lunch. Skirty Marm made her intellectual face, and opened a magazine called *Woman's Weekly*.

"I've written the vicarage phone number on top of Old Noshie's head!" shouted Mr Babbercorn. "If you get into trouble, just look under her wig!"

Slowly, the train began to move. The vicar and the curate waved until their arms ached. Mr Babbercorn stared after it until it was no more than a speck on the horizon.

"I *want* to trust them," he said gloomily, "but they've never been to a big city before, and you know how silly they can be."

"Mrs Miller did her best, but they still look absolutely bonkers, even in those clothes!" groaned Mr Snelling. "Oh, why have we let them do this?"

Mr Babbercorn sighed. "We must be bonkers ourselves, but what else can we do? We're counting on them to reverse that spell and bring Alice back!"

After they returned from the station, the vicar and the curate were too busy to be anxious. The bishop was coming for lunch, and the vicarage looked like the laboratory of a mad scientist. They had to work quickly to clear away all signs of spell-binding. Mr Snelling gathered up all the lost things that had arrived by mistake and took them into his study to sort through. Mr Babbercorn hid the witches' cauldron and wiped away the peculiar spillages.

He was sweeping a heap of dried spiders' legs into the dustpan when there was a loud knock on the back door. He opened it, and found himself staring up into the face of a gigantic woman.

She was nearly three metres tall, and nearly as wide. A shawl hid the lower half of her face, but the part you could see was incredibly ugly. She was holding a tray of red apples. Her mean little eyes glittered at Mr Babbercorn.

"Buy an apple, young reverend sir!" she wheedled. "Will you buy an apple to help a poor old woman?"

"I . . . I . . ." stammered Mr Babbercorn. Everything about this woman froze his blood. He knew why when her shawl fell down suddenly, revealing her mouth.

It was full of *metal teeth*!

"These are magical apples, young sir," cackled the old woman. "One bite and your dreams will come true!" The shawl fell further, revealing her chin.

It was covered with a *thick grey beard*!

At last, after all he'd heard about her, Mr Babbercorn was face to face with the wicked ex-queen of the Witches – Mrs Abercrombie

herself. His knees trembled and he felt the colour draining from his face, but he made his voice as strong as he could.

"Reverse that spell and give back my Alice, you inhuman FIEND!"

The change that came over Mrs Abercrombie's face when she realized she had been rumbled was very nasty. She stopped pretending. Her tray of apples vanished. And her smile turned into a hideous snarl.

"All right, so you're not as daft as Snow White, and you won't fall for the apple trick." She took a step nearer to the trembling curate. "You know what I want – and you'd better obey me if you want to see your Alice again. I've come for the Power Hat!"

"I . . . I haven't got it!" squeaked Mr Babbercorn. Which wasn't true – the Hat was in the spare bedroom upstairs, wrapped in an old sheet. He didn't dare think what would happen to his witches if the ex-queen got her hands on it.

"I know it's here," growled Mrs Abercrombie. "And I know your witch pals and that wretched cat-slave are away. You have no magic to protect you now!"

Mr Babbercorn did the only thing he could think of. With all the strength he could muster, he slammed the back door in Mrs Abercrombie's face.

"Locks and bolts cannot keep me out!" she thundered through the door. Her voice was deep and gravelly and seemed to shake the foundations of the house.

Mr Babbercorn hurtled upstairs to the spare bedroom and locked the door behind him.

"Good gracious!" he gasped. He rubbed his eyes to make sure he wasn't dreaming. Yesterday, the Power Hat had been covered with an old sheet. Today, it was covered with a cloth of gold, richly embroidered and studded with precious stones. The curate had never seen anything so beautiful – where had it come from? There was no time to wonder.

Downstairs, he heard a crash, followed by the voice of Mr Snelling.

"My good woman, what does this mean? How dare you smash down my back door? Leave my house this instant – OW! *Put me down*!"

Heavy footsteps came plodding up the stairs. Mrs Abercrombie was coming to claim her

Power Hat – and she would kill anything that stood in her way.

"Oh, crumbs – I know who you are now!" cried the voice of Mr Snelling, in sudden terror. "Cuthbert, don't let her in!"

This advice was pointless. Mrs Abercrombie bashed down the locked door as if it had been made of wet tissue paper. She was carrying the vicar over her shoulder.

"AT LAST! AT LAST!" she cried, with a great roar of triumph. "Months of work and all my fortune, but I've found my Hat! I am queen once more! Oh, come to me my proud beauty, and together we will reign in WICKEDNESS!"

She threw down the vicar (luckily, he landed on the spare bed) and tore aside the golden cloth that had recently been an old sheet. Her face lit up with horrible joy – and then an extraordinary thing happened.

Quick as lightning, the Power Hat leapt on to the head of Mr Babbercorn, burning a large hole in the ceiling. Mrs Abercrombie screamed and tried to snatch it back. But it wouldn't come off. She tugged, she pulled, she heaved. The Power Hat was stuck fast to the bewildered curate's head.

Mr Babbercorn now understood why Skirty Marm hadn't enjoyed wearing the Hat. It made his brain feel several sizes bigger, and so crammed with knowledge that it was about to burst. He shut his eyes and the strange letters appeared in the blackness inside his head.

Don't give me to that MONSTER! typed the Hat. *I don't want to be used for WICKED-NESS ever again. I have heard the playful sporting of the Brownies, and the wise counsel of the Old Folks' Club, and they have made me long to change! I have learnt how GOOD humans are, and I want to STAY!*

"Is that why all the strange things have been happening around you?" asked Mr Babbercorn. "The huge flowers, and our terrible choir singing like angels? Not to mention that old sheet turning to gold."

YES, typed the green letters. *These are the things I do now – I create sweetness and beauty. Think of all the beautiful things we could do together! Tell Mrs Abercrombie to GO AWAY. She has no power over you as long as I'm stuck to your head!*

Mr Babbercorn felt rather foolish, but did as he was told.

"The Hat says – well, I'm afraid it wants you to go away."

Mrs Abercrombie stamped her foot so hard that all the ornaments fell off the mantlepiece.

"I'LL BE BACK!" she screamed. "You've stolen my property! The Power Hat is rightfully MINE!"

And in a puff of black smoke that smelt of cabbage, she vanished.

Mr Snelling slowly got off the bed. He was shaking all over. "Bless my soul, that thing has discovered goodness! It wants to come and live in our village!"

Downstairs, the front doorbell rang.

"Oh dear," Mr Babbercorn said. "The bishop."

"You can't wear the Power Hat all through lunch with the bishop!" Mr Snelling was horrified. "He'll either think you've gone crazy, or he'll find out we're keeping witches on church property!"

"But I can't take it off!" protested Mr Babbercorn. He knew he couldn't possibly face his bishop in a two-metre-tall witch's hat with a candle at the tip.

He closed his eyes. "Hat – can you make

yourself look a little less strange?"

Certainly, typed the Hat. In half a second, it had changed itself into a small, woolly bobble hat. The hat was black, and the bobble was white.

"At least it's a *clergyman's* bobble hat," said Mr Snelling, relieved. "I'll tell him you've got a cold and you have to keep it on. But I wish I knew how the witches and Mendax and Alice were getting on in London!"

7

The Keepers of the Gate

"We're doing just *marvellously* so far," said Skirty Marm. "I can't think why the Vicar and Mr B. made all that fuss."

The witches were having the time of their lives. They had managed a thrilling journey on a train, an even more thrilling ride on the top of a red London bus, and now they were standing in front of the chocolate counter at Fortnum and Mason's.

It was five minutes before closing time, which was part of the plan. The famous shop was emptying, and the smart shop assistants were starting to close up their gleaming counters for the night. Some of them were looking curiously at the two peculiar old ladies with the cat basket, but they were far too polite to comment.

The voice of Mendax floated out of the basket, in a complaining mew. "We're supposed to be hiding – don't just stand there gawping!"

Mendax hadn't been having such a thrilling time. He'd been stuck in the cat basket with Alice all day, forbidden to speak in case a human heard him.

Old Noshie and Skirty Marm were still staring with open mouths at the magnificence around them. Skirty Marm took off her sunglasses to get a better view. It was an impressive sight, even for a human – great heaps of fruit, slabs of cheese, wonderful painted tins of biscuits and teas, and bottles of rare wine. It was nothing at all like the food hall at Maggot's, the only department store on Witch Island, where there was hardly anything for sale and you had to biff the assistants if you wanted to be served.

Mendax's voice reminded them they were here on a mission. Mr Snelling had drawn them a map of his favourite shop and suggested the basement as a good place to hide. Making sure nobody saw them, the witches scuttled down a grand staircase and found themselves in the hampers department, where big baskets of delicious food were sent out to customers. As the vicar had predicted, the biggest hamper was big enough to hide two witches and the cat basket. Its wicker sides creaked alarmingly as they climbed inside.

"It's a bit of a squeeze in here," complained Old Noshie.

"Serves you right," said Mendax. "Now you know what it's like to be shut in a basket."

"Let's not argue," peeped the tiny voice of Alice-the-Snail.

The others all remembered how terribly she wanted to stop being a snail, and how sad Mr Babbercorn would be if she stayed one. This made them very still and quiet, and Skirty Marm resisted the temptation to say something crushing to Mendax. Gradually, silence fell around them. The voices and footsteps seemed to go on for a very long time, but at last they were alone in the empty shop.

"Right," said Skirty Marm, clambering out of the hamper. "Let's get started." She put her sunglasses and her knitted hat into Mrs Miller's handbag. "Now, I'm going to try an aperture location spell to see if I can find the entrance that Professor Mouldypage talked about. We don't want to be stuck in here all night."

"I wouldn't mind," said Old Noshie, looking

hungrily at a pile of fruitcakes in tartan tins.

"You promised not to nick any food," Mendax reminded her smugly.

"We're not here to eat," Skirty Marm said impatiently. "The aperture location spell should lead us to the secret entrance to the Gardens Before Time, and then we can grab those berries Professor Mouldypage told us about."

Something had been worrying Old Noshie all day. Now that they were so close to the secret entrance, she couldn't help blurting it out. "Skirt – what did the Professor mean, when she said it might cost more than we were prepared to spend? I don't like the sound of that at all!"

"It probably means we have to pass some sort of test, or answer a tricky riddle," said Skirty Marm, who never liked to admit she didn't know something. "Don't worry – I'm brilliant at riddles."

"Supposing it's something dangerous?" quavered Old Noshie.

"Oh, it's bound to be dangerous," said Mendax. "I expect you'll have to walk through flames or over a bed of knives – or perhaps deal with a fierce dragon who might bite off your heads—"

"Shut up!" Skirty Marm stamped her foot. "It's too late to worry about the dangers now!"

She opened the cat basket. Mendax leapt out of it, with Alice-the-Snail clinging to the top of his head. Alice trembled as she watched Skirty Marm mumbling a long spell. Skirty snapped her fingers, and Alice gasped to see a round white light, about the size of a ping-pong ball, hovering in mid-air.

"It's searching," Old Noshie explained. "It's the aperture finder, and it will locate any magic within a radius of seven miles."

They all watched the white light anxiously. It moved slowly across the carpeted floor, over several glass cases and a large polished counter. Then, even more slowly, it came to a halt against a wall. It hung there for a moment, quivering like a dog sniffing, then dropped to the floor.

It stopped beside a metal grating in the wall and suddenly began to fizz like a firework, before disappearing in a shower of sparks.

"Hurrah!" yelled Skirty Marm, dancing a jig of excitement. "We've found it! That's the entrance!"

"But you'll never get inside that little hole!"

cried the tiny voice of Alice, in alarm. "You're miles too big!"

"My dear Alice," Mendax said, "you have a great deal to learn about magic. The witches will simply perform an elementary shrinking spell. I used it myself, to sneak out of the enemy camp at Fungus Gulch—"

"Shut up!" snapped Skirty Marm. She was trying to remember the shrinking spell, and secretly wishing she could look it up in her Red-Stocking Spellbook, which she'd had to leave behind on Witch Island.

Her first attempt shrunk everything except the witches' feet – Old Noshie let out a tremendous wail when she found her small body standing over a pair of feet as vast as a couple of tugboats.

Skirty Marm dealt Old Noshie a quick biff on the end of her huge shoe, which was the only part of her friend that she could reach. "Pull yourself together!" she ordered sternly.

Then Skirty Marm corrected her spell, and the witches' feet caught up with the rest of them. Their heads were now level with the worried snail clinging to Mendax's fur. The black cat himself looked the size of a carthorse beside them.

Together, they wrestled open the metal grating in the wall. Mendax slid his sleek cat's body through it. Alice clung on harder.

"I'm in a sort of pipe," Mendax said. His voice sounded strange and echoing. He sneezed. "Excuse me. It's rather dusty in here."

"Come on, Nosh." The shrunken Skirty Marm pushed Old Noshie through the grating, scrambled after her, and closed it behind them.

"It's awfully dark," squeaked Alice.

"You'd better light your finger, Skirt," said Old Noshie. "Whenever I try to do it, I end up setting fire to my wig."

Skirty Marm held out her finger, and a clear flame shot from the top of it. The dark pipe was flooded with light. The four of them stared at each other's frightened faces.

"What do we do next?" Alice-the-Snail asked fearfully.

"Walk on!" cried Skirty Marm. "Walk on, and the entrance will reveal itself!"

"You'd better climb on my back," said Mendax. "Please don't wriggle."

Skirty Marm vaulted easily up the cat's slippery black sides. Old Noshie was not such a good climber, and there was a delay while she was pulled up by her friend. It was extremely strange to be sitting on Mendax's smooth fur.

Very carefully, Mendax inched forward inside the metal pipe.

"Stop kicking!" he hissed crossly. "And there's no need to pull my fur out in handfuls!"

"I'm not!" protested Old Noshie. "How would you like it, if – OW!"

Without warning, the metal pipe seemed to melt from under Mendax's paws. The four of them were falling, falling, falling, into a pit of darkness. Old Noshie's borrowed wig flew off. Skirty Marm lost one of her human shoes. Still they went on falling, until they seemed to be plunging towards the very centre of the earth. It became very cold, then oddly warm.

At last, with a jolt that tumbled the witches off Mendax's back in a ragged heap, they landed on something hard.

They were in a dark underground cave, its walls and ceiling hidden by thick shadows. Something was gleaming at them, very brightly. When their eyes adjusted they saw a huge pair of golden gates, like spiders' webs, glistening in the flickering light of hundreds of candles.

Skirty Marm's eyes were round with awe. "The gates to the Gardens Before Time! No living witch has seen this incredible sight!"

A voice suddenly rang out, making the friends jump out of their skins. "Greetings, travellers!"

The voice was deep and rough, but strangely squeaky – and definitely not human.

"Welcome to the Chamber of the Order of the Good Rodents!"

Mendax turned white under his black fur. "Rodents? That means *rats*! They'll tear us to pieces!"

"Fear not, cat," said the voice. "You are safe with us."

Now they all saw that the darkness was studded with hundreds of pairs of beady eyes. They were surrounded by huge grey rats that were almost as large as Mendax. Alice screamed and shot back into her shell. Mendax cowered behind the two shrunken witches, who couldn't help looking nervous.

The largest of the rats stepped out into the candlelight. He wore a suit of rather rusty chain mail under a moth-eaten grey robe. His long tail was wrinkled and his whiskers were white with age, but his old voice was strong.

"We are the Order of the Good Rodents," he said. "Our Order was founded many thousands of years ago to guard this underground entrance to the Gardens Before Time. The Power Hat has prepared us for your coming."

"Power Hat?" muttered Skirty Marm, surprised. "Why on earth would it help us?"

"The Hat is not acting by itself," said the Chief Rat, in a deep and solemn squeak. "At the moment, it is stuck to the head of a very good young curate. He has ordered the Hat to help you. For this reason, we have waived the usual penalty."

"Eh?" gasped Old Noshie. There were too

many long words for her to understand.

The Chief Rat looked at her sternly, from beneath his bushy white eyebrows. "Know this, witch – usually, the berries from the Backwards tree are only given in exchange for a life. If you did not have such powerful friends, we would have been allowed TO EAT YOU."

Old Noshie's green face paled. "We taste horrible – don't we Skirt?" she said quickly.

"Now we know what the professor meant," said Skirty Marm, frowning. "Smelly old bag – she might have warned us properly!"

The Chief Rat turned his beady eyes towards her. "Would you have acted differently if you had known the true danger?"

"No!" Skirty Marm said bravely. "We'd do anything for Alice and Mr B. – we wouldn't even mind being eaten by rats!"

"Speak for yourself," muttered Mendax. "Personally, I'd have liked to be consulted first."

"You have our word," said the Chief Rat, "that you will not be eaten. This snail may enter the garden and remove two berries from the Backwards tree."

"Hooray!" cried Old Noshie. "Come on, Alice!"

The Chief Rat shook his grizzled old head. "The snail must enter on her own. Only she can be allowed to see the gardens – and live."

The witches and Mendax looked doubtfully at Alice, who seemed very small and delicate inside the circle of large grey rats. The little snail, however, came fully out of her shell and extended her horns. "Don't worry about me," she squeaked. "I'm not scared!"

"You love this curate," the Chief Rat said. His stern voice softened. "And your love will protect you as long as you remember to touch nothing else in the Gardens Before Time. Be warned, human female – if you even stop to rest on the way, you will stay in the gardens *forever*!"

"Oh, Alice, be careful!" wailed Old Noshie.

"I'm ready," said Alice bravely.

Alice found that she could move a lot faster than usual as she followed the Chief Rat towards the gleaming gates. He patted her shell once with his paw and unlocked the gates with a huge golden key. The witches and Mendax watched her sliding away alone into the shadows.

Skirty Marm nudged Old Noshie hard. "Stop crying!" she whispered, sounding cross because she was trying not to cry herself. Neither of them would ever forget the sight of tiny Alice, vanishing into the unknown.

"We will wait," said the Chief Rat. "Do sit down. And do have a biscuit – we get them from upstairs."

It was a long, long night. The witches and Mendax sat for uncountable hours, surrounded by silent staring rats. The biscuits were delicious, but even greedy Old Noshie was too anxious to enjoy them.

"Don't mind the others staring at you," said the Chief Rat. "They don't see many strangers."

"I'm not surprised!" snapped Mendax. "Word is bound to travel if you normally eat your guests!"

At last, the gate swung open. Old Noshie and Skirty Marm burst into cheers when the small snail emerged, carrying two purple berries in her horns. They rushed over to her.

"Are you all right?" cried Skirty Marm. "What happened?"

Alice-the-Snail's face was smiling in a dreamy dazed way.

"It was perfectly beautiful!" she sighed. "The

gardens are so sunny and quiet – I saw some angels having a picnic!"

"Yes, it's a popular spot," said the Chief Rat. "But I'd be grateful if you didn't tell anyone the details."

"I don't think I could if I tried," said Alice. "Thank you for being so kind to us."

For the first time, the Chief Rat smiled, his long sharp teeth gleaming in the darkness. "Don't mention it. Always a pleasure to oblige the Power Hat. And anyway, we've enjoyed it. You're the first visitors we've had in eight thousand years."

Alice said, "You must be awfully old!"

"As old as time, my dear," said the Chief Rat. "I watched time being wound up – and I'll stay here, guarding these gates, until it winds down."

Alice bowed her horns respectfully. "You've been very good. I'll never be mean about rats again!"

"Don't get carried away," said Mendax sourly. "Most of them are dreadfully common."

This seemed to amuse the old rat. "Cats and rats are not friends in the lands where time rules."

"The time!" cried Skirty Marm suddenly. "The vicar and Mr B. will be so worried! We've got to change Alice back!"

"We will escort you upstairs," said the Chief Rat. "Good luck – and if you want to send us a slice of your wedding cake, just drop it down any drain in Piccadilly."

8

Old Noshie's Dream Comes True

The journey back to the surface was so fast that it left them all breathless. They fell out of the grating in the hampers department in a heap, and Skirty Marm immediately changed herself and Old Noshie back to their proper sizes.

"Pity," remarked Mendax. "I liked you smaller."

"Now for the level six transforming spell," said Skirty Marm, ignoring him. She looked in Mrs Miller's handbag at the watch the vicar had lent her (Old Noshie hadn't been trusted with it because she couldn't tell the human time yet). "We'll have to be quick – there's only about an hour before the shop opens!"

Deciding this was an emergency, the witches borrowed a saucepan from the store's kitchen department and dashed around the shelves of the food hall snatching various ingredients.

"It's a good thing the professor said to leave out the warts," puffed Old Noshie, "because I don't think they have any!"

Skirty Marm had to concentrate very hard to perform the spell backwards, from end to beginning. The mixture in the saucepan looked disgusting – grey and curdled, with bits of squashed spider and grated geranium leaf floating on the scummy surface. Skirty lit all the fingers of her right hand and stuck them under the saucepan to bring it up to the boil. Mendax, Old Noshie and Alice watched, hardly daring to breathe, as she dropped in the two magic berries.

Above them, a door slammed.

"Someone's coming!" squealed Old Noshie. "Quick!"

As the mixture in the pan started to bubble there was a deafening crash, like a clap of thunder. It shook everything in the shop, and they felt the shudders deep in the earth beneath them. This was Mrs Abercrombie's locking charm unlocking. The blast sent the borrowed saucepan flying, and blew the friends off their feet.

While the witches were still coughing and

spluttering in the cloud of grey smoke, a woman's sweet voice cried, "Good gracious! I'm back!"

Mr Babbercorn and Mr Snelling hadn't slept a wink. They had sat up in the vicarage kitchen all night, drinking tea and trying to keep their spirits up. Both nearly jumped out of their skins when the phone rang.

"I knew it," groaned Mr Snelling. "It'll be PC Bloater – they've all been arrested! How are we going to explain this to the bishop?"

Mr Babbercorn answered the phone, and for the first time since Alice's transformation he laughed with joy.

"Alice!" he shouted.

Alice and her friends were at the station in Tranters End. Skirty Marm had made them all invisible to get them out of Fortnum and Mason's (and the man who opened the shop never could explain the huge explosion or the disgusting saucepan).

The vicar and the curate jumped into Mr Snelling's car and zoomed off to meet them. The other passengers on the small country station were amazed to see a young curate wearing pyjamas, a dog collar and a bobble hat dancing up and down the platform with two crazy old ladies, a cat and a woman in a blue dress.

With tears in her eyes, Alice hugged the witches and Mendax.

"How can we ever thank you all?" she cried. "Oh, Cuthbert – why on earth didn't you tell me about your magical friends straight away? They're WONDERFUL!"

Old Noshie and Skirty Marm were beaming. This was the proudest moment of their lives.

Mr Babbercorn gave them each a kiss. "It was stupid of me to hide you. I hope you'll forgive me."

The vicar sniffed and kissed Mendax – he loved the bossy little cat very dearly.

"Wait till you hear our adventures!" he said. "That blessed Power Hat wants to live in Cuthbert's underwear drawer! It wants to be good, and it will never give itself to Mrs Abercrombie again!"

"It seems to have taken rather a fancy to me," said Mr Babbercorn, smiling. "I've made it promise not to turn my vests into gold, like it did with the old sheet. Ordinary curates don't wear golden vests."

"Too itchy," put in Mr Snelling. "It says it'll prove its new goodness in quieter ways in future – and it's rebuilt my extension!"

Alice stroked Mendax and took the hands of the witches.

"Cuthbert," she said, "I'd like Mendax to sing a solo at our wedding. And I'd like these two lovely witches to be my bridesmaids!"

Old Noshie opened her mouth to say something – and not a sound came out. Her dream had come true.

Three weeks later, on a sunny summer afternoon, Mr Babbercorn and Alice were married. Mr Snelling took the service, with his round face wreathed in smiles. Every single person in Tranters End was crammed into the church.

"Don't they make a beautiful couple?" whispered Mrs Tucker.

Mrs Miller chuckled. "And don't those witches look a treat?"

Old Noshie and Skirty Marm walked behind the bride, holding up the train of her long white gown. Bridesmaids usually wear frilly dresses, but these hadn't been thought suitable for two rather wrinkled witches. Instead they had new velvet dresses, with matching velvet-covered pointed hats. Skirty Marm's were bright blue, to set off her purple hair. Old Noshie was in tasteful salmon-pink, to tone with her green skin. They each carried a bouquet of thistles and dandelions.

Mendax, who was very proud of his new white collar, sang "O For the Wings of a Dove" (licking his lips, because he was fond of a plump dove).

"Skirt," said Old Noshie, "I'm the happiest witch in the world!"

"Me too," said Skirty Marm. "Pooh to Mrs Abercrombie – she can't touch the Power Hat now it wants to hide here. And she can't touch us, as long as it's here to protect us!"

Professor Mouldypage had sent a gleeful radio-message, telling them that the former queen had spent all her witch money on the locking charm and had now taken a job teaching at Yellow-Stocking School to make ends meet.

"So we'll all live happily ever after!" said Old Noshie.

When Mr and Mrs Babbercorn left for their honeymoon in Gusty Bay, Alice threw her bouquet of pink roses into the crowd – and Skirty Marm caught it.

Mr Snelling giggled. "That means you'll be the next bride!"

"Not likely," said Skirty Marm with a broad grin. "Being a bridesmaid's good enough for me." She bit the head off a rose. "DEE-LICIOUS!"